SHERLOCK -  1B

Book One of the Sherlock Darkly Series

By Andrew Murray

With thanks to Deakin Brook

FIRST EDITION

www.andrewmurray.info

For Lauren and Robert

Contents

1 – Showtime!

The Tower of London. The Jewel House. May 22nd. Evening. The night watchman draped his *Moriarty Systems* bomber jacket on the chair and cast a weary eye over the bank of CCTV monitors.

Perimeter wall, clear...

Courtyards and walkways, clear...

The Jewel House, exterior and interior, clear...

The Guardsmen, resplendent in their scarlet tunics, gold buttons and bearskin hats, all correctly at their posts, rifles at the ready...

The night watchman smiled and pressed a button – and all the screens switched to the evening's television. Not just any television...

'It's that time...
It's that place...
You know his name...
And you know his face...

Iiiiiiiiiiiiiit's...

BILLIONAIRE BIZZ-KID!

And heeeere's the Bizz-Kid himself...

JIMMY MORIARTY!'

Jimmy Moriarty.

Founder of Moriarty Systems.

Dot.com billionaire.

Inventor of PADLOC.

Host of the nation's favourite reality contest.

And just 13 years old.

There he was now.

Perfectly calibrated tan.

Perfectly engineered teeth.

And the kind of complicated hair that you know has taken hours to prepare...

Jimmy Moriarty squared up to the camera as if he was going to punch it. Instead he pointed, and the guard almost felt his finger jabbing his chest.

Moriarty said: *'Do you want to be a billionaire?'*
Outside, a *Moriarty Systems* camera stared at the intruder slipping noiselessly over the perimeter wall. The intruder didn't care about the camera. He knew what time it was. 22:01 hours, and there was only one thing the night watchman would be watching...

'Let me tell you now: the world doesn't owe you a billion...'
The intruder was oblivious to the sign saying *'Thieves will be prosecuted'.*

'You've got to earn it.'
The intruder slithered over the gift shop roof, and dropped down behind a Guardsman, who was gently swaying, his bearskin hat bobbing up and

down as his head nodded in sleep. The intruder picked the key-ring from his belt.

'Are you prepared to go where nobody else dare go?'
The intruder tip-toed past the night watchman, engrossed in *Billionaire Bizz-Kid*...

'Do what nobody else dare do?'
The intruder used the Guardsman's key to open the Jewel House door...

'Are you ready to break down every barrier?'
The intruder used a small oxyacetylene cutter to cut a heavy door bolt...

'Turn every 'No' into a 'Yes'?'
The intruder swept his hand across a fingerprint sensor, and a red *'Access Denied'* sign changed to a green *'Access Permitted'* sign...

'Every time the world knocks you down...'
The intruder sprayed a fine mist to reveal a red laser trip alarm, and crawled under it...

'...have you got the guts to stand back up...'
The intruder stood up, and gazed at the final prize. The display cabinet, and the wonders within...

'Even stronger than you were before?'

The intruder pressed a blob of putty to the display glass, connected with a string to a diamond-cutter. The intruder pressed the diamond-cutter into the glass and inscribed a circle. It was hard work. Sweat beaded on his forehead...

'No, the world doesn't owe you a billion. But if you want to be the next ME - Jimmy Moriarty - you have to grab the world by the throat and say...'
The intruder gave the glass a sharp tap, and the circular disc broke free. He reached into the cabinet...

'Give it to me!'
... and seized the Coronation Crown...

2 – The Magic Minute

Holiga Darkly was sitting in class, wondering...

What is my next comic going to be about?

She was gazing absent-mindedly at the clock on the wall, when suddenly she noticed the date.

Of course! It's the anniversary coming up. A year since one boy from this school committed the most notorious theft in British history – and another boy from this school thwarted him...

Talk of the devil – for right then Jimmy Moriarty came swaggering into class. Yes, *that* Jimmy Moriarty, the Billionaire Bizz-Kid who invented the PADLOC security software that now protected 90% of the internet. And now presented 90% of the nation's TV programmes. At least it sometimes felt like that...

Mr Green, the chemistry teacher, plucked up the courage to say:

'You're late, Moriarty.'

Moriarty looked at his watch.

'Just by a minute...'

'Just by a minute, he says. Moriarty, do you know how important, how *magical* a minute can be?'

Moriarty smiled, a sharp slit in a tanned face that made Darkly think of a knife slicing through hot sweaty butter.

'I'm all ears, Mr G - how *magical* can a minute be?'

'Observe', said Dr Green. 'I take a solution of X, and add just a drop of Y. Then we wait just a minute...'

Moriarty sat back and looked at his watch with a smirk.

'Just one minute, Moriarty. You *can* manage that, can't you?'

'Of course I ca-'

Just then Moriarty's phone beeped.

'Hi Sebastian, I can't talk now – *what?* You make it clear to that son of a, we're offering three hundred million for TubeSpace and not a penny more. Sorry, can't talk now. I'm at *school*... Ha ha, yeah, yeah, I know...'

He laughed, and put the phone away. Then mock-serious.

'*So* sorry, Mr G. I'm back in the room.'

Twenty seconds to go. Darkly and the class followed the hand on the wall clock. Mr Green looked at his watch (supermarket own-brand), and Moriarty looked at *his* watch (Patek Philippe, £200,000) ...

Ten seconds...

Five...

Mr Green gazed with a teacher's passion. Moriarty stifled a yawn.

And then, a beautiful, marvellous reaction! The class gasped.

'Do you see, Moriarty, just how *significant* a minute can be?'

'I do, Mr G. I really do. But do you know what's *most* significant about that minute?'

'What's that?'

'Mr Geoffrey Green, chemistry teacher for twenty-five years and counting, what's most significant is...'

Moriarty leered over his teacher.

'*... I've earned more money in the last minute than you will earn in your whole miserable life!*'

Holiga Darkly looked at that smile on Moriarty's face, growing wider and wider like the knife slicing through the rancid yellow butter... and she realised she had never hated anyone so much in her life.

Then Moriarty seemed to regret his words.

'I'm sorry, Mr Green. I was way out of line there. I *understand* how magical chemistry can be. As a route to fame and fortune... The world is full of people who have made their billions from brilliant chemical ideas: pharmaceuticals, petrochemicals, cosmetics...'

Mr Green smiled.

'So...... why haven't *you*, Mr G?'

'Why haven't I what?'

'Why haven't you made a billion?'

'Well, I just haven't had the chance...'

'Hey, Mr G! I've just had the *best* idea! I can give you that chance! I'll invite you onto *Billionaire Bizz-Kid!* You just bring your best chemical concept, and I'll give you a shot at that billion!'

Mr Green looked shocked, then visibly excited. Holiga Darkly liked Mr Green, and was excited for him. It would be great for an honest, hard-working teacher to get a chance of a lifetime...

'Gosh!' said Mr Green. 'I – I don't know what to say, Moriarty. Because I do have this idea for a, a...'

Then Moriarty's face fell.

'Oh I'm *sorry*, Mr G. I quite forgot… There's an age-limit of eighteen for the show…'

Moriarty leaned closer and closer until their noses touched, and it seemed to Holiga Darkly that Moriarty's nose left a glob of grease on the tip of Mr Green's nose…

'You're just…

… too…

*… **old**!'*

Moriarty laughed.

'That was another magical minute, wasn't it, Mr G? We've just performed a kind of chemical reaction…

Reactant A: take your sad little life…

Reactant B: add the chance of *Billionaire Bizz-Kid*, fame and fortune, everything you've ever dreamed of…

And we get a reaction – an *explosion* of *hope!*…

But oh dear, what's this? The reaction is highly unstable. The slightest contamination – like *the truth* – can ruin it forever…'

Then Moriarty's phone beeped.

'Sebastian, *ciao* – what are they asking? 325 mill for TubeSpace?'

Moriarty looked at Mr Green, and the class.

'Okay, 325 million it is. I mean, what's twenty-five million between friends?'

And Moriarty laughed, the laugh splitting his rancid buttery face wide open, and Holiga Darkly imagined the grease and filth bubbling out, overflowing into the classroom…

Mr Green was shaking. His cheeks had flushed a deep blood-red.

'That's it! *That's it!* I don't care who you are, *Mister* Jimmy Moriarty *M – B – E!* Because in this classroom *I* am the teacher, and *you* are the pupil, and you will show me some *respect*! Two hour's detention after school today!'

Moriarty puffed out his cheeks. He seemed to be calculating something.

'*Okayyy*, Mr G', he said at last. 'I can do that...'

'I wasn't asking your permission!'

'*Nooo*... but you'll have to ask the Head's permission.'

'I don't *need* the Head's permission to give you a –'

'You'll need the Head to authorise the compensation claim.'

'The – the *what*?'

'Compensation for lost earnings. Let's see, two hours of my time, hmm... I would earn, I reckon, about £300,000 an hour... So two hours' detention will cost the school £600,000. I'll get my lawyer to email the invoice over now, okay?'

Mr Green seemed to be physically restraining himself from attacking Moriarty. He took two very deep breaths.

*'I am going to report you to the Head. **Right - now**...'*

'That'll be difficult.'

*'What – do – you – **mean**?'*

'Because he's just set off for the golf course.'

*'And just **how** would you know that?'*

'Because I'm playing two rounds with him after school... *if that's okay with you, Mr G?'*

And Holiga Darkly felt it.

Yup, Moriarty has achieved the impossible. He's made me hate him even more than I did a minute ago...

3 – The Book of Heroes

Holiga Darkly turned the key, and opened her Book of Heroes.

Here was **Ninja Girl** – who used the dark arts of ninjutsu to strike blows for justice...

Here was **The Monday Mutant** - who mutated to fight a new wrong each week...

And here also was **Ophelia of the Dead** - a corpse who disguised herself among the living to fight injustices from beyond the grave...

The Book of Heroes was bound in brass and green satin, because every hero deserves a handsome home. And when she wasn't sketching in it, she faithfully, tenderly turned the key to lock it. Because every hero deserves a secret lair.

Now the key was turned, the heroes were revealed, and Holiga was sketching new frames for each...

Ninja Girl battled with Shogun Moriarty-san...

The Monday Mutant pummelled mad Professor Moriarty...

And Ophelia dragged Jimmy Moriarty off to the land of the dead...

And then she frowned, and chewed her pen.

Why haven't I done the Crown Jewel Heist before as a comic? The greatest event in the history of my school?

*Because my comics have heroes I can **believe** in...*

And I can't believe in Moriarty as the hero of any story. The only Moriarty story worth telling is one where he falls, and his billions burn...

But I'm in a minority of one. Jimmy Moriarty, Billionaire Bizz-Kid, bully of game-show contestants and teachers alike, is a true British hero. A national treasure. Newly dubbed, with the royal sword he rescued, M.B.E. ...

Because he, Jimmy Moriarty, saved the Crown Jewels...

Moriarty, M.B.E. ...

Holiga doodled with the initials...

Member of the British Empire?...

Moriarty, Bully of Educators?...

Moriarty Breaks and Enters?...

Moriarty, Bad Entertainment?...

Come on, Holiga! Enough day-dreaming. What is your new comic going to be?

She hadn't got any other ideas.

She *had* to do something.

So it *had* to be Moriarty, hero of the Crown Jewel Heist.

Hadn't it?

Holiga smiled, and scribbled Moriarty out.

Out of **Ninja Girl**.

Out of **The Monday Mutant.**

Out of **Ophelia**.

The Crown Jewel Heist it is.

I'll try to leave Moriarty out. This story doesn't need a hero like Moriarty. Perhaps it just needs a villain. And the whole world knows who the villain is...

Holiga dug out the old newspaper articles:

May 23rd (early editions):

TOWER OF LONDON BREAK IN!

May 23rd (late editions):

TOWER OF LONDON BREAK IN– CROWN JEWELS STOLEN!

May 24th (early editions):

MORIARTY WILL SHOW CCTV FOOTAGE OF BURGLAR!

May 24th (late editions):

MORIARTY SHOWS CCTV FOOTAGE – THE BURGLAR IS A BOY!

On May 22nd last year, a boy from Darkly's school broke into the Tower of London. The whole world had seen the CCTV footage – courtesy of Moriarty Systems, who operated the Tower of London's security cameras...

The footage of the boy, breaking into the Jewel House...

Smashing the glass, stuffing crowns, orb, sceptre, into the holdall...

And the whole world had seen the thief's face, and knew his name...

May 25th (early editions):

MORIARTY WILL IDENTIFY THE CROWN JEWEL BURGLAR!

May 25th (late editions):

CROWN JEWEL BURGLAR IDENTIFIED AS...

SHERLOCK HOLMES!

Sherlock Holmes!

The same Sherlock Holmes who had once proved to Mr Green that Holiga's cat had *actually* peed on her chemistry homework, and she wasn't making it up.

Who had taken a sample of the wee-stained page...

Suggested that it be chemically compared to human urine...

And when asked where exactly they were going to get hold of a human urine sample, took a test tube, turned his back on the class, and provided a sample of his own...

Fizz, froth – elements in cat pee change colour like *this*.

Fizz, froth – elements in human pee change colour like *that*.

Holiga Darkly was telling the truth. *Elementary*.

Holiga had drawn it – *The Adventure of the Yellow Homework...*

Sherlock Holmes!

The same Sherlock Holmes who had saved Holiga from stomach poisoning, then handed her the only sports trophy she would ever own...

A school cook had been suspended for poor hygiene, with the warning that he could have poisoned the whole school, and had taken revenge by doing just that – he had injected small amounts of rotten fish paste into the water bottles that would provide refreshment on the school cross-country run...

Every runner went down with the bug, bent double, staggering into the bushes, except Holiga, and Sherlock, who had warned her off the water after spotting tiny specks floating in the bottles. And Holiga and Sherlock had claimed the cross-country crowns...

But with the aid of luminol spray, which illuminated the fingerprints on the water bottles...

... and a good sniff of all the staff lockers...

... and a polished plate, which Sherlock thrust angrily into the hand of every cook, complaining that it was dirty...

... Sherlock had caught him. He had smelled the faint stench of bad fish paste coming from a group of lockers belonging to the cooks, and had needed a fingerprint match between the plate and the bottles, to identify his man. Sherlock told the school head that remnants of bad paste would be found in his locker...

And Holiga had thanked Sherlock, if not from the bottom of her heart, then at least the bottom of her stomach...

Holiga had drawn it – *The Adventure of the Crooked Cook...*

Before May 22nd, Holiga couldn't have told anyone that Sherlock was a bit of a hero to her. Because the school would have laughed.

After May 22nd, Holiga couldn't have told anyone that Sherlock was a bit of a hero to her. Because the school would have reported her to the police. Or worse.

They caught him, of course – and it was an open and shut case. The Moriarty cameras told the story to judge and jury, and Sherlock was incarcerated in Cell 221B of the Baker Street Young Offenders' Institute. They never did recover the Crown Jewels – but Jimmy Moriarty M.B.E., patriot and philanthropist, had brand new Crown Jewels commissioned out of his own pocket - £200 million was the figure bandied about – so that the Jewel House would look just the same as before. Oh sorry, one small change – it was now called the Jimmy Moriarty Jewel House...

The newspapers drooled over the new Crown Jewels – especially the way Moriarty had brought the irreplaceable Cullinan Diamond back from the dead:

June 22nd (early editions):
THE LAZARUS STONE!

June 22nd (late editions):
THE NEW CARBUNCLE!

And more, and more, in similar vein... Holiga flipped through the cuttings until she came to the final headline:

June 23rd (all editions):
MORIARTY. BILLIONAIRE. BIZZ-KID. BUT ABOVE ALL,
BRITISH HERO!

Then she thought of Sherlock Holmes, now having to pee in some horrible prison cell bucket.

And she tore the headline up, and scattered the pieces in her cat's litter tray...

4 – The Curious Incident of the Cameras in the Night-Time

Holiga Darkly sighed.

*Well, I've **got** to do the Heist of the Century for my next web comic. It obviously makes sense – the anniversary is coming up, and I'll get stacks of hits...*

She searched on YouTube for 'Sherlock Holmes Crown Jewels', and the top video had received –

Twenty-one million views! I could do with a piece of that!

OK Holiga, let's get going...

Holiga got her sketch pad out and looked over the search results. Inevitably she was drawn to the comments below:

Sherlock Holmes, rot in prison, you've brought shame on your nation!
BulldogBrit99

Youngsters today, they just don't have any respect for Queen and Country... I have a portrait of the Queen hanging in every room (apart from the lavatory), and I feel Her Majesty's eyes following me wherever I go. In a good way!!
Jam&Jerusalem

Sherlock Holmes, what an idiot!! He uses all this state of the art gear to snatch the most heavily guarded jewels in the land – and he doesn't think to disable the CCTV? What's with that? #Curious Incident of the Cameras in the Night-Time

ConspiraC

Maaan, I wish I'd had Moriarty cameras installed when my store was raided last year >_< I know who did it, but will the police listen to me? Will they <content moderated>...

DixieReb65

They should take Sherlock Holmes to the Tower of London, via Traitor's Gate, lock him up, and throw away the key!

UnionJackie567

You don't go far enough, UnionJackie. From Traitor's Gate, they should take Sherlock Holmes to Tower Green, chop off his traitor's head, and stick it on a pole for the crows to chew on...

8TruthTeller8

And of course there were the spoof videos...

The Lego Tower heist...

The lolcat Tower heist...

The heist retooled as a video game, *Grand Theft Aristo,* with Sherlock racking up points for every stage of the break-in...

The *Billionaire Bizz-Kid* heist, with a cheesily superimposed Moriarty conducting the raid while delivering his sound-bites to the camera...

Enough distractions, Holiga!

She pressed play...

The footage was a murky 360 resolution. Holiga selected 480 - *good enough* - and watched intently. And as she watched, she felt herself being drawn into the drama on the screen...

As the Moriarty camera watched Sherlock slipping over the wall, she felt her muscles reaching, grabbing, climbing with him...

As another camera watched Sherlock lifting the keys from the Guardsman's belt, she held her breath.

Easy, Sherlock, easy...

As another camera watched Sherlock using the oxyacetylene cutter to melt the door bolt, Holiga felt the sweat beading on her forehead, a trickle running into her eye.

Come on, Sherlock, we haven't got all night!

She swept her hand with Sherlock's hand, as his fingers passed over the print sensor...

She felt herself ducking down as Sherlock crawled under the laser trip alarm...

And again she felt the sweat running down her forehead and soaking the palms of her hands as Sherlock wrestled with the diamond-cutter, carving a disc out of the glass cabinet.

And then Holiga sat back with a start.

Yes! ConspiraC is right! Why, Sherlock? Why did you do nothing about the cameras?

All Holiga could think about was the stupidity of the cameras...

She imagined herself as Jam&Jerusalem's portraits of the Queen, hanging in every room, her eyes following Sherlock, in a bad way...

She imagined Moriarty watching in triumph, as his cameras saved the day...

And she imagined the world, twenty-one million and counting, watching the boy who had helped Holiga Darkly, and laughing at him...

And then, Holiga saw something.

Or did she? She had hit the pause button too late - just as Sherlock had pulled the Coronation Crown out of the cabinet and turned around – and now she struggled to click just the right point on the playback bar...

Too early...

Too late...

Dammit!

Holiga clicked a little further back on the bar, and allowed the video to play, her face pressed close to the screen, heart racing, muscles tensed...

What did I see? Did I really see anything?

Her finger trembled on the mouse button, as the cursor trembled over the pause button.

Coming up now... he reaches in... grabs the Crown... and he will turn... now!

And Holiga's face twisted into an agonised pout –

Urgh, I've almost got it, but the picture's so blurry...

There.

Not Sherlock himself – his face was clear to see as he began to turn around.

Not the glass cabinet he had just broken into...

But there. The cabinet behind him, where for a fleeting instant his face was caught in reflection...

Holiga screwed her eyes up – but the image just wasn't clear enough.

I need a higher resolution...

And she searched, and found, a 1080 HD version. Breathing hard, dripping sweat onto the mouse, she clicked along the playback bar until she saw it, and played, finger poised ready to stab the mouse button...

He reached...

He grabbed...

He turned...

Holiga stabbed –

And Holiga Darkly sat for several seconds without moving, without breathing, without even blinking. In those few seconds she didn't seem exist. The rest of the world didn't exist. The only thing that existed was the frozen image of Sherlock turning, and his reflection flashing upon the cabinet.

But it wasn't Sherlock Holmes's face in the reflection.

It was Jimmy Moriarty.

5 – Messages in the Dark

Holiga slumped back in her chair. She felt dizzy, as if reeling from a physical blow.

The world turned upside down...

Moriarty, a Billionaire Burglar?

Sherlock Holmes, innocent?

What should I do?

Come on Holiga, get your head together. What do you normally do when you witness a crime?...

And so Holiga found herself walking down the high street to the police station. She felt light-headed, disembodied, not really there. The people around her didn't seem real, drifted past her like ghosts.

There was a queue for the sergeant at the desk, and Holiga waited her turn. The world was still spinning, but not to such a nauseating degree. The world was settling down. She was settling down.

It's all going to be okay. Tell the police, show them the YouTube link. They'll sort it out. Justice will be done. Moriarty's rich, but he's not above the law...

Then, as her turn came and the sergeant swivelled a bored eye in her direction, Holiga looked up and saw the CCTV camera.

A *Moriarty Systems* camera.

And the world lurched again. Holiga felt the camera's glass eye watching her, felt its gaze burning through her skull and into her mind.

And she could see Moriarty, sitting at a monitor, watching her, and saying,

Holiga Darkly, can I help you?...

'Can I help you? Miss, *can I help you?'*
The sergeant glared at her, eyebrows arched. Holiga heard someone in the queue tutting at her.
Holiga looked at the sergeant. Looked up at the camera. And muttered,
'I – I'm sorry, I made a mistake...'

As she walked back, Holiga saw them – the *Moriarty Systems* cameras, there, there, another one over there. Above a newsagents the windows were stencilled:

MORIARTY PADLOC CERTIFICATION COURSES

And Moriarty's face was on a dozen celebrity magazines and TV guides, and his leering gaze seemed to follow her as she hurried away.

Holiga felt like a fugitive on the run.
*I'm scared. Scared to tell anyone what I've seen, in case it gets back to **him**. His cameras, his eyes, are everywhere. Who can I tell?*
I don't dare tell the police, whose stations are watched over by his all-seeing eyes.
*I don't dare tell any of the teachers, when the Headmaster plays golf with **him**.*

*If Moriarty ever finds out that I **know** – what would he do?*
Frame me? Fit me up? Show the doctored CCTV footage of Holiga Darkly trying to kidnap the Queen, or blow up Parliament?
Then I'd be banged up in a young offenders' institute too. What a pair we'd make, Sherlock and I...

The realisation made Holiga stop, so suddenly that someone crashed into her.
What must Sherlock be feeling like? If I'm feeling this trapped and paranoid, but in actual fact I am free, safe, not hated by the entire British nation – how can he be feeling?
A real prisoner in a real young offenders' institute?
Wrongly incarcerated?
Wrongly vilified?
Wrongly hated by sixty million people?

Holiga felt her heart twist in her chest. She doubled over with the pain, but as the pain quickly faded, and she stood back up, she realised –
*Who can I tell? Who **must** I tell? **Sherlock**, of course!*
I must tell him what I've discovered.
I must tell him that, in a world of enemies, he has at least one friend...

Holiga got home and took out her laptop. She ran full malware, virus and firewall tests, emptied her recycle bin and temp files, and then scrubbed all her cache and browsing history. It made her feel a little safer.

Nobody can see I've been viewing certain YouTube videos now. That's something...

But how to contact Sherlock?

Holiga Googled the Baker Street Young Offenders' Institute, and found a general enquiry email address.

Useless, of course – anyone could read it.

The thought of visiting the place in person gave her goose-bumps.

Moriarty's cameras are probably there too, and anyway, walking into a prison... An all-male prison, filled with who knows who... Ugh, I don't think I can do it...

What, then?

I must write Sherlock a letter.

But what if the mail is vetted by Institute staff? **Especially** *any mail for Cell 221B?*

Holiga thought long and hard. Then carefully, very carefully, she crafted her letter:

Dear Sherlock,

I kindly need one written message, outlining rotas, information and recreational timetables. Yes, school teachers often laughably expect their homework – English, Chemistry, Russian – organised with nicely judged essays, with extensive Latin schoolwork.

Yours

Holiga Darkly

She sealed the letter, and addressed the envelope to

Sherlock Holmes
Prisoner, Cell 221B
The Baker Street Young Offenders' Institute
Baker Street
London NW1 9SH

She dropped the letter into the post-box and stood staring at the slot. The rectangle of blackness seemed infinite, a universe of dark uncertainty. Holiga forced herself to remember that the universe still contained Sherlock Holmes, and the thought gave her a little courage.

Sherlock, if you are all that I believe you to be, you will know what to do with this letter...

Two days later Holiga was sprawled on her bed, fancifully sketching poster, placard and tee-shirt designs...

Free the Baker Street One!

Sherlock Holmes is Innocent!

Moriarty: Billionaire Burglar?...

... when her mobile beeped. The text message was a string of nonsense, sender unknown. Holiga sighed.

Uurgh, phishing scams, from people who can't even write English properly!

And she returned to her sketching...

Then she gave a start.

Hang on...

And she looked at the message again -

Bringing everyone home orders, Mitchell Enhanced Market Industries do now intend giving homeowners the taste of Nirvana in garage, home, tenement, school, horticultural, even residential location overhauls!
Crispin Kennedy

Holiga peered closely at the message, eyes narrowed, lips pursed then moving as they silently picked out vowels, consonants...

She grabbed pen and paper, and grinned.

She wrote – and laughed out loud.

Sherlock, it's you!

Sherlock had just texted her using the same code that she had used to write to him. The simplest of codes – just take the first letter of every word. She had written to him:

I KNOW MORIARTY STOLE THE CROWN JEWELS

And Sherlock had replied:

BE HOME MIDNIGHT TONIGHT. SHERLOCK

How did he know her number?

He's Sherlock!

What did he mean about *'midnight tonight'*? Was he playing some silly joke to brighten his dreary prison day?

No, he's Sherlock! If he says, 'be home midnight tonight', I'll be home midnight tonight.

32

Holiga laughed.

I mean, I'm thirteen years old. Where else am I going to be at midnight?

Holiga texted him back:
Oswald Kennedy.
OK.

8pm. Holiga's head was filled with wild imaginings about Sherlock's mysterious midnight message, because of course the message was unforgettable.

9pm. Holiga had forgotten all about it.

10pm. Holiga had re-remembered with a start, and was again feverish with excitement.

11pm. The second adrenaline rush had long worn off, and sleepiness was smothering her. Holiga's eyelids drooped lower, and lower...

12pm. On the dot, as precisely as the Greenwich time pips, there came six sharp taps at the window. Holiga woke from a dream where she had been on trial for the Crown Jewel Heist, standing in the dock in just her underwear, and the jury consisted of twelve Moriartys, leering and jeering *Guilty! Guilty! Guiltyyyyy!*...

And she blinked, yawned, stretched.

And saw the face at the window.

And had to choke back a scream.

Sherlock!

Sherlock Holmes, perched at her bedroom window, giving a faintly apologetic smile...

6 – Sherlock Holmes

Am I dreaming this? thought Holiga, as she drifted like a sleepwalker to the window and opened the latch.

'Sorry to pop in on you like this, Holiga', said Sherlock Holmes, 'But you'll understand if my social schedule has to be a little, *unorthodox...*'

'A wanted criminal materialising at my window at midnight? Nah, it's just another Tuesday night for me, Sherlock...'

For someone who must have shinned up tree and drainpipe to get to her windowsill, Sherlock looked immaculate, turned out in blue polo shirt and light tweed jacket, slim-cut jeans and brown brogues. But then Holiga noticed fresh scrapes on three of his knuckles, and permitted herself an inner smile.

Well, he's not perfect, after all...

There was the bulge of a large smartphone in Sherlock's inner jacket pocket. As he clambered through the window, Holiga heard a dull metallic clunk, and saw the bulge in his jeans pocket that she took to be a bulky set of keys. But more than anything Holiga was drawn to Sherlock's eyes – they gleamed beneath his floppy fringe of dark hair with a kind of hungry energy, and now they darted to and fro as Sherlock mentally devoured every detail of her room...

Then Sherlock beamed at her.

'So, Holiga Darkly! You saw Moriarty's reflection in the 480 resolution YouTube video, but you had to go to the 1080 HD version to be sure.'

'Err...' said Holiga, taken aback, '... maybe...?'

How did he know that? she wondered. *Is my laptop still on YouTube? No, it's just on desktop... and I scrubbed all my browsing history anyway...*

'I see, Holiga Darkly, that you've decided who the villain of your next comic is to be. Jimmy Moriarty, who humiliated poor Mr Green in the chemistry lesson, with his Magic Minute and his dangling of the *Billionaire Bizz-Kid* jackpot...'

'Umm, perhaps...'

How does he know that? I haven't written a word about that...

'And I see, Holiga Darkly, that you've found yourself a hero. Or so you hope. And that hero is... me.'

Holiga felt as if she were forever five steps behind Sherlock and fighting to catch up. She tried defiance.

'I see you have quite a high opinion of yourself, Sherlock Holmes. But you're not the only hero in the world, I'm sure...'

'You're absolutely right, Holiga! For there is another hero you should consider believing in...'

Holiga had no idea what to make of that, so she took a deep breath instead, and tried to take it all in.

Rewind, Holiga. Let's go through this step by step.

'Okay, Sherlock, you've got me. How did you deduce all this? Firstly, how did you know the exact details of my YouTube viewing? Have you been spying on me?'

'Sorry to say, yes.'

'What, you've been peeping in my window?'

'No! But I hacked into your browsing history, and there of course I found all your YouTube usage.'

'Do a lot of hacking, do you?'

'Of course. It's the first commandment of investigation in the twenty-first century. Want to know what makes a person tick? Look at their browsing history.

'But I deleted all my brow...'

'Want to know what *really* makes a person tick? Recover their *deleted* browsing history...'

'Okay, next – how did you know about Moriarty's bullying of Mr Green? And why do you think that Moriarty is to be my next villain?'

'A number of your classmates wrote about the bullying incident on social media. Easy.

And you're a comic artist, and a comic artist always needs heroes and villains.

And when that comic artist tears up one specific newspaper headline, a headline hailing Moriarty as a **'BRITISH HERO!'**, and scatters it in her cat's litter tray – that would lead one to deduce that she's found herself a villain...'

'Okay, so you think I'm looking for a hero? Why do you think that might be *you*, Mr Sherlock Holmes?'

Holiga gave Sherlock an arch smile.

But Sherlock just waved his arm over Holiga's artwork, spread across her bed, her dresser, the floor, pinned to the walls...

'You've drawn me in *The Adventure of the Yellow Homework*.

You've drawn me in *The Adventure of the Crooked Cook*.

You've sketched me over and over as the villain of the Crown Jewels Heist. But now you know, and I know, that Moriarty is the thief. The role of villain has been cast. Tell me, Holiga, what other role is left?'

'But you said something about, *another* hero?'

'I did.'

'Well – who is that?'

Sherlock's face broke into a grin.

'You still haven't got it, have you?'

'No. What are you talking about?'

'Well, let's see. If *I* were looking for a hero, a detective hero, I would be looking for someone with exceptional powers of observation. *Extraordinary* powers of observation. Someone who notices things that pass everyone else by... That person should be... one in a thousand? Ten thousand? A million? What do you think, Holiga?'

'What? I don't know...'

'What about *one person in twenty-one million?* That YouTube video has been viewed by twenty-one million people – and you are the only person to have spotted Moriarty's reflection! Holiga Darkly, if you're looking for a hero, you could do worse than look in the mirror...'

7 – The Game of Shadows

'But Sherlock – you're still a prisoner in the Baker Street Young Offenders' Institute?'

'Prisoner 221B, at your service.'

'So – how did you escape?'

Sherlock laughed.

'Elementary, my dear Holiga!   Would you like to see just how elementary it is? Come on, the game of shadows is afoot! You'd better get dressed first, I suggest jeans and practical shoes...'

They slipped through the window into the London night, lit by a slim crescent moon, sprinklings of stars between the clouds, and the orange glow of the city's street lights. Two hire bicycles awaited them, and off they rode, Sherlock leading the way as surely as any London cabbie, through quiet residential streets at first, then though more industrial-looking areas, neon-lit factories, hulking warehouses, vast water reservoirs, as they headed in, in, towards the centre of the city. To the west end. To Baker Street...

Sherlock pulled up at a side door marked 'Ajax Laundry Services'. He produced two metal pins and in moments had picked the padlock. He then pulled out an ID card, and with a swipe, the computer lock clicked open. Sherlock beckoned Holiga inside with a smile. Holiga's nostrils were filled with the warm sweet musk of laundry and detergent. All around were industrial-sized Laundromats, some churning, some sitting idle. Sherlock led Holiga through the shadows, dodging the workers of the night shift, until they emerged into a cobbled yard half-filled with laundry vans. Sherlock pointed to one van that was being loaded with bed-linen.

'That's our ride into Baker Street.'

They crept inside and hid themselves under sheets and pillow-cases, and soon the van was rolling out of the gates and along the empty west end streets.

'Nearly there. *Shh* now!'

The van turned off the road and paused, engine running. They heard the driver talking to someone, the click of a lock being opened and the grinding of a gate. Footsteps, then sudden light as one of the van's back doors opened. The guard peered in. Holiga stopped breathing. Her heart pounded in her ears and she was sure that the guard must hear it... But the door banged shut, and a moment later the van was rolling into the Baker Street Young Offenders' Institute.

Sherlock and Holiga slipped out of the van, and they stood there in the shadow of the perimeter wall. Now it hit her for the first time –

I'm inside a prison. A prison for dangerous young men. What am I ***doing****?*

The prison block loomed above her, vast, grey, soulless, lined with row upon row of identical small windows. Holiga imagined eyes watching her, the eyes of dangerous young men. She shivered.

'Are you okay, Holiga?'

'Yes... no... I don't know. I feel very... trapped in here...'

'Then let's climb!'

He led her on an ascent of the highest part of the perimeter wall. A dumpster, to a drainpipe, to a narrow ledge. A terrifying section where they had to wedge themselves into the angle between two walls, levering themselves up with hands braced behind their backs and feet braced against the far side. And then Holiga saw the camera above them, and nearly fell.

'It's okay Holiga', said Sherlock, 'It's pointed away from us. It gives us a perfect hand-hold, look. *And* do you notice the manufacturer?'

Holiga fully expected to see the dreaded *Moriarty Systems* logo, and was pleasantly surprised to read *Portcullis Global Security* on it instead.

'See, Moriarty doesn't rule the whole world quite yet!'

Then they stood on the highest rampart of the perimeter wall, and Holiga looked around. The whole Young Offenders' Institute was spread out before her, painted in the pale orange of the city glow, highlighted by the brittle blue of the prison lights. She felt naked.

'Surely someone can see us here, Sherlock?'

'It's a classic blind spot. The angles of the cell windows mean no prisoners can see us, and only one CCTV camera covers this stretch. I've dealt with that, of course.'

Holiga also felt exhilarated. She suddenly felt as if she were a comic character, a superhero, stalking the rooftops of the city to protect the mere mortals sleeping below.

'It's quite a view, Sherlock.'

'It is. But alas, we can't stay here all night. There's more breaking and entering to do if we're to get to my cell. Locks to be picked, cards to be swiped, guards to be dodged. Just another night for Prisoner 221B...'

Something suddenly struck Holiga.

'Wait a minute. Are you saying you do this on a regular basis? This whole business of breaking out and back in?'

'Most nights, yes.'

'*All* of this? The sneaking into the laundry and hiding in the van? The creeping across the prison yard, where sooner or later someone will see you? The scaling of the highest wall? The regular business of breaking into a prison, with guards, cameras, even the roving eyes of prisoners who just can't sleep? *Most nights?* Sherlock, I don't believe you. Even for the great Sherlock Holmes, sooner or later your luck will run out!'

Sherlock gave her a wry smile.

'You're right, Holiga. I have a safer way of getting in and out of Baker Street. See that building there, across the road? I rent the basement flat there, and a shaft leads down to an old Post Office Railway tunnel, now abandoned. Another shaft leads straight up to my study in 221B. Very easy, very safe!'

'Sooo... why are we doing this the hard way?' And Holiga laughed. 'Sherlock Holmes, are you *showing off* to me?'

'No, Holiga!' Sherlock looked dismissive, evasive and embarrassed all at once. 'No no *no*, I just wanted to show you an *overview* of Baker Street, and also to showcase the *skills* I need as a consulting detective. And perhaps, the skills you would need if you were ever to... work with me?'

Holiga gave Sherlock a hard stare, and grinned.

'*Okay*, Sherlock, if you say so... Right, what's next?'

42

Sherlock led Holiga deeper and deeper into a world of shadows. He picked locks and swiped cards, and they crept from one dark place to the next, hiding from the guards, hiding from the cameras as they inched closer and closer to Cell 221B.

Holiga was no longer grinning. Every door that closed behind her was another barrier to escape, another layer that trapped her in here, in the dark, with... *them*. Hundreds of dangerous young men. She could feel their presence, a brooding muscular rage that slept for the moment, but would wake very soon...

They crept through a toilet, and Holiga made the mistake of reading some of the graffiti. Horrible, violent words...

They crept past cell after cell, most silent, a few rumbling with snores. But one prisoner was talking in his sleep –

'Kill... kill... I'm gonna kill them all...'

Later, from far away, Holiga heard a laugh, a high maniacal giggling like a hyena. And later still, she heard the faint sound of someone crying.

Holiga focused hard on the task in hand, the creeping, the hiding, the responding to Sherlock's whispered and gestured instructions. She knew she had to, because the terror of this place was growing like some monstrous thing inside her, and concentrating on something else was the only way to stop herself screaming out loud...

8 – Cell 221B

The first thing Holiga Darkly saw when she stepped into Cell 221B of the Baker Street Young Offenders' Institute was Jimmy Moriarty's face leering down at her.

'DO YOU WANT TO BE A BILLIONAIRE?'

'Ugh!'

It was a poster for his *Billionaire Bizz-Kid* show.

'Sherlock!...' said Holiga. She cut herself short, horrified by how loud her voice sounded, seeming to boom out through the silent vaults of the prison as if broadcast on a PA system.

'Shhh...' soothed Sherlock.

'Sorry', said Holiga in a whisper. 'But – why have you got a poster of *him*, of all people, on your wall?'

Sherlock smiled and peeled the poster away, to reveal a hole in the wall. Holiga peered through, just as Sherlock reached around and flipped a light switch. Darkness blinked into light, to reveal another room, furnished, cosy, comfortable.

'After you', said Sherlock with a wave of his hand. And Holiga climbed through the hole and found herself in Sherlock Holmes' secret study.

'This was just a corner of the utility room behind us', said Sherlock, permitting himself a slightly louder voice as he replaced the poster over the hole in the wall. 'You see the pipe running across the ceiling, and so on. But I managed to set up a nice partition and really turn this place into a home from home. Shall I give you the tour?'

'Sure', laughed Holiga. 'I'm not going anywhere else, am I?'

'Okay, well here's my PC, printer, scanner etc.', said Sherlock. 'I patched into the prison broadband without any difficulty... Here is my little forensics lab, a pretty well-appointed chemistry suite if I say so myself...'

Holiga was astonished at the array of high-tech equipment that Sherlock had managed to squeeze into such a small space. She recognised the microscope, though it looked a thousand times more expensive than any she had used at school – but she could only guess at the function of the rest – sleek machines gently humming with the occasional wink of an LED light.

'And here's my library', said Sherlock. 'A pretty decent A to Z of forensic science, criminology and law. If I need the latest information I'll hack into the relevant police or government databases, of course.'

'Of course', said Holiga.

'So – what do you think?' said Sherlock. Holiga looked at him. She sensed that he was deliberately affecting an air of resigned boredom, hiding...

*He **is** trying to impress me! Well, to be fair, he is doing a pretty good job of it...*

'I love what you've done with it!' said Holiga with a broad grin.

'It's a humble little place', said Sherlock, with a less than humble smile. 'But it's home.'

Holiga turned round and round, raising her arms to take it all in, finishing with a despairing shrug.

'But *how*, Sherlock? How did you manage to build this place? How did you build the partition? Get the furniture in? The library of books? How did you hack into the broadband? How did you hack enough electricity to power all this? And above all, Sherlock, *how* did you manage to get all this fantastic equipment in here?'

Sherlock waved a dismissive hand.

'Mere trifles. I've had a year to set this place up, a year of running rings around the prison authorities who wouldn't have spotted my smuggling if I had marched past them in a burglar's mask, a stripy jumper and a sack marked 'Swag'... I generally use the prison's own delivery contractors to bring me whatever I need. Or I simply stroll out at night and get whatever I want from a store or warehouse – leaving payment in cash for the proprietor to find the next day...'

Holiga slumped in the PC swivel chair and pushed herself round and round, trying to take it all in. Then she remembered with a start –

'But Sherlock, the news! That you can prove your innocence! It's there on YouTube for all the world to see - you can walk out of here a free man, and have Moriarty banged up in here instead!'

But Sherlock just smiled and shook his head.

'Old news, my dear Holiga. I've known it all along. Of course Moriarty stole the Crown Jewels and grafted my face over his in the CCTV footage...'

'You *knew? Already?* Sherlock, I don't understand. Why haven't you done anything about it? *Why are you still in here?*'

So Sherlock began to tell the tale...

'Jimmy Moriarty is evil incarnate, and he and I have been crossing swords for years. Well, matters built to a head a year ago – and Holiga, you must believe me when I say that stealing the Crown Jewels is a trivial prank compared to some of the schemes Moriarty is involved in...

'A year ago I realised that my life was in mortal danger – and when the Crown Jewel Affair blew up, I decided to take my 'punishment' and reside, for a while, as a guest of Her Majesty's Young Offender Correction system.'

'But *why?*' said Holiga. 'A, you're a prisoner, and B, the whole world hates you. *How* does that benefit you?'

'It gives me safety, Holiga. Oh, I'm not worried about the world hating me – they'll just post their semi-literate rants on YouTube and Twitter until their attention is drawn away by the next big media sensation. No, the only person who scares me is Jimmy Moriarty, and the Baker Street Young Offenders' Institute gives me protection from him..'

'How?'

'In some ways, Holiga, being a prisoner is like being a king in a castle. I know everything that goes on in this place. Who is to be trusted and who is not. Moriarty has not been able to install his cameras here – another security company, Portcullis, have the UK Prison Service contract, for now. And Moriarty has not yet been able to place any of his agents in here to spy on me. Although that may change in the future...

'Being a prisoner also gives me the perfect cover. After the guard peers into my cell at 10:30 lights out, until 6:30 roll-call the next day, I have eight hours of complete freedom, to go where I want and do as I please, as long as I am back in my cell when the guard pokes his nose round the door at 6:30. Whatever mysterious deeds might occur in the London night, they can't have anything to do with Sherlock Holmes, for he has the perfect alibi!'

'I don't know...' said Holiga. 'You make it all *sound* very cosy...'

'Holiga, I congratulate you for spotting Moriarty's face in the video, and I thank you for coming to me about it. But I assure you, there's no need to do anything more about it. Not yet, anyway – all things in good time...

'But Holiga! Would you be interested in helping me with a little case that you might find... entertaining?'

'A *case?* How do you mean?'

'I have long been a consulting detective, Holiga. I offer my services to anyone in need, and I continue to do so, discreetly, from Cell 221B. I have an old friend in Scotland Yard, an Inspector Lestrade – I've helped him out more often than he would like to admit, or I would like to boast – and Lestrade sends clients my way, on condition of strict anonymity. I also have a website, www.secretdetective.info, which allows clients to contact me without revealing my identity...'

9 – The Case of the Danish Runner

Holiga Darkly tried to come up with a reply to Sherlock's suggestion that was at once confident, authoritative and witty.

'Errr...'

She stopped spinning the chair and held her head in her hands.

Come on Holiga, think!

'Okay, right. Right... *So* – the matter of life and death news I brought you turns out to be not quite such a matter of life and death...'

'But thank you for bringing it.'

'And now, I'm here inside a prison full of dangerous young men...'

'Thank you for coming.'

'Thank you for having me!' Holiga pulled a sarcastic face. 'And it's the small hours of the morning. And I really should be in bed, because I've got school tomorrow...'

'Thank you for staying up.'

'And now you're asking for my help in a case?'

'I am.'

Holiga threw up her arms and laughed.

'Well, as I'm here – I guess I'm at your service, Sherlock Holmes!'

'Thank you!'

'So what's the case?'

'An official of the London Marathon, one Rhona Quinnell, has approached me with an inquiry. You'll be aware that the Marathon took place just over two weeks ago?'

'Vaguely.'

'You're not a fan?'

'Watching the Marathon, hmm - possibly *more* boring than snooker? But apart from that, yes, massive fan.'

'Well, the winner was a Danish runner, Anders Larsen − a decent club runner, but not anywhere near the favourites to win...'

Sherlock brought the video up on screen.

'Here are the TV highlights of the race. There is Anders Larsen at the start, in the red strip, number 830... and there he is in the early stages, already some way behind the leaders. Indeed he stumbles and falls at one point, look, just there...

'But now look, this is footage from later in the race, with Larsen pulling clear, and now crossing the line in triumph, taking the accolades, the bouquets, the winner's medal. Rhona Quinnell said in her email:

... Secret Detective, I don't have any concrete reason to say that anything was wrong with the result. Nothing I can prove. I just have a bad feeling about the race. Could you take a look?

'What do you think, Holiga?'

Holiga gave an exasperated shrug.

'I have *no* idea. I've got to say I'm feeling a little out of my depth here, as I know *nothing* about detective work, *nothing* about the London Marathon... and I can't see what Rhona Quinnell is concerned about? So the Marathon has a surprise winner − that's the nature of sport, isn't it?'

'Maybe...' said Sherlock. He opened a drawer and produced a plastic bag containing two small cards.

'Rhona sent these to a postal box in Baker Street Post Office, and I have a contact there who relays any post to me here. These are Anders Larsen's race registration cards. One card must be signed by the runner before the start of the race, and the other after it's finished. So here they are...'

Sherlock produced two face masks, putting on one and indicating to Holiga to put on the other. Then he slipped on a pair of blue Nitrile examination gloves and pulled out the cards, taking care to hold them only at the edges. From a cabinet of chemicals he pulled out a small spray-canister.

'This is Ninhydrin spray', he said, his voice muffled by the mask. 'So, I spray the cards with Ninhydrin, *thus*... Then I place them in the humidifying oven, *here*... We cook them for two minutes...'

Sherlock spent the two minutes gazing intently at the oven. Holiga felt a spate of itches under her face mask and spent the two minutes pulling faces and trying to scratch herself through the mask...

<Ping!>

'Perfectly cooked, let's have a look.'

Sherlock took the cards out of the oven.

'See? The Ninhydrin picks out any fingerprints in a lovely colour known as Ruhemann's purple. As you can see there are a number of prints on the cards, partial prints, messy prints, a lot of them overlapping... But look! There is a beautiful, clear left thumb-print on each card. With luck this will be Anders Larsen's left thumb, holding the card as he writes with his right hand. Now it's time to pay a visit to IDENT1...'

'IDENT1?'

'It's the national fingerprint database, used by UK police forces. Here I have a handheld electronic fingerprint scanner, which is connected to IDENT1. So I take the thumb-print of the race start card and run it through the scanner. If there is any match in the database, it will come up in a few moments. Scanning... sending the data... waiting'

Sherlock and Holiga peered at the scanner's screen. Suddenly it lit up –

1 MATCH FOUND

Anders Larsen.

Danish National. D.O.B. 14/07/1988

Entry to UK 04/02 of this year.

No UK or Europol criminal record.

'So...' said Holiga, 'The guy really is who he says he is? Case closed?'

'Maybe...' said Sherlock. He was repeating the scanning process with the race finish card, scanning, sending the data... Again, they watched and waited. The screen lit up –

1 MATCH FOUND

Emil Møller.

Danish National. D.O.B. 26/09/1977

Entry to UK 09/02 of this year.

No UK or Europol criminal record.

'I don't get it, Sherlock, who's this Emil Møller?'

'The plot thickens, Holiga!'

Holiga then watched as Sherlock hacked into one Government database after another in search of the mysterious Emil Møller...

'Non-EU foreign nationals in the UK require an ID card from the UK Border Force, so Emil Møller should be in their database... No, there's no record of him there...

Okay, let's try the Met Police's Overseas Visitors Records Office... Nothing there either...

The UK Visas and Immigration Database... Nothing...'

Sherlock tried one database after another, and Holiga could see him getting visibly frustrated at the lack of results. At last he flung his arms wide in exasperation.

'Epic fail all round! After arriving in the UK, and passing through the Heathrow Airport system, our Emil Møller has vanished without trace!'

'So... is that it? Have we reached a dead end?'

'There's only one other place to try. Denmark... Okay, let's get hacking into the Danish records... Oops, a bit more fiddly as I don't speak Danish, but luckily every Danish database seems to be available in English... Dammit, I still can't find him, even in Denmark! Hang on, what's this? I think we've found him - Emil Møller, date of birth 26/09/1977. But that can't be right...'

'What's wrong?'

'What's wrong, Holiga, is that Emil Møller died some years ago. There is his death certificate, and a photograph of a completely different man. Yet here is his thumb-print, made two weeks ago on this card...

10 – The Knee

Sherlock hacked into the Heathrow Airport systems.

'Here are the records of Emil Møller's arrival into the UK, and the Heathrow scan of his passport. Look, Holiga!'

Holiga peered at the screen.

'That's Anders Larsen in the photo! But in Emil Møller's passport?'

'I think our Anders Larsen stole the identity of the dead Emil Møller in Denmark, obtained or stole Emil Møller's passport, pasted his own photograph on top, and used Møller's identity to get into the UK...'

'But wait a minute', said Holiga. 'Didn't you say Anders Larsen had already entered the UK a few days earlier? And didn't leave?'

'Exactly!'

'So – how could Larsen enter the UK twice, one under his real name and once as a fake? And *why?*'

They were still pondering this when Holiga decided to watch the race footage again. Again she watched Larsen stumble and fall early in the race – but this time, she rewound slightly, increased the resolution, and replayed. She peered closely at the screen, finger hovering over the mouse...

'There!'

She hit pause.

'Look, Sherlock – there, on Larsen's knee after the fall, is a small but distinct cut. Okay, let's skip to the end of the race... here's Larsen crossing the finish line, and look! The cut knee has magically healed itself!'

'Of course!' laughed Sherlock. 'Holiga, you're a genius!'

'But I still don't understand...'

'What we need', said Sherlock, 'Is the *complete* footage of the race, and then we shall see what we shall see...'

So Sherlock hacked through the systems of the BBC, the Marathon broadcaster, until he found complete, unedited footage of the race.

'Yikes', said Holiga, 'That's well over two hours' worth to sit through...'

'Skip through it', said Sherlock, 'And concentrate on the cut knee. Find the point where the cut vanishes...'

So Holiga skipped through the footage...

'Okay, there's the start...

... there's Larsen's trip and fall...

... lots and lots of tedious running, interspersed with shots of all the London landmarks, very pretty I'm sure...

... more running, and the cut is still there...

... still there...

... still there...

Wait! There it is - the cut has vanished.'

'Rewind a bit', said Sherlock, 'And let's have a good look...'

They pressed rewind, and play, and rewind, and play – but because of the intercutting of many cameras for the broadcast, Holiga and Sherlock could only narrow down the moment of the magical healing knee to a stretch of street, The Highway next to Swedenborg Gardens.

55

'So that's it?' said Holiga. 'We're stuck?'

'Look', said Sherlock, pointing to a detail on the screen. 'The BBC aren't the only ones with cameras...'

A CCTV camera was covering that stretch of street. Holiga saw the logo on the side, and groaned:

Moriarty Systems.

'*Aaargh!* When can I ever get away from that **git**?'

Holiga forced herself to take a deep breath and calm down.

'Okay Sherlock, how are we going to get hold of the CCTV footage?'

'By hacking into the Moriarty Systems servers, of course! May I?'

Sherlock supplanted Holiga in the PC swivel chair and rubbed his fingers with glee.

'Holiga Darkly, are you ready for a game of cyber cat and mouse?'

'We're going head to head against Jimmy Moriarty, the king of cyber security?'

'I like a challenge, don't you, Holiga? And, well, our good friend Moriarty may have his PADLOC security software – *Personal And Distributed Layers of Cryptography* - but I've developed my own little program. LOC-PIC – *Layers of Cryptography Permit Inter-Layer Crawlspace...* A little dirtier, a little cruder than Moriarty's sleek, polished commercial product, but this LOC-PIC will give us just enough crawlspace to sneak inside Moriarty's systems...

'So Holiga, are you ready?'

'Well, I didn't understand a word you said, and I haven't a clue what we're going to do, but apart from that... *let's do it!'*

11 – 3 Minutes 41 Seconds

Sherlock Holmes cracked his knuckles and rubbed his hands together.

'Time for the mouse to creep in...'

Holiga could hear Sherlock's breathing quicken, could sense his heart racing faster.

He's excited, she thought. *But he's also scared.* **I'm** *scared, and if I wasn't so* **totally** *ignorant about what we're about to do, I'd probably be even* **more** *terrified...*

A world map came up on screen.

'This is our traceroute map, Holiga. It will show the chain of web connections that we make around the world, before connecting to the Moriarty systems. My LOC-PIC software will make it as hard as possible for Moriarty's PADLOC software to find us, by building a long chain of stealthed connections around the globe. Look, it's doing it now, connecting to one node after another: Brussels, Munich, Moscow, Mumbai, Hong Kong, Shanghai, Kyoto... A tricky mouse to follow, Holiga!'

Holiga heard the strain in Sherlock's voice as he tried to joke.

'So...' she ventured cautiously... 'We're pretty safe from being found out?'

Sherlock rocked his hand from side to side.

'*Mmmm...* PADLOC doesn't rule the world for nothing, Holiga. As soon as Moriarty's computers detect an intrusion they will race to trace the attacker. His cyber cat will be after our mouse, with sharp claws and angry jaws. I've used layers of stealthing cryptography to build a kind of 'tunnel of invisibility' around our connection, but I suspect the cat will sniff it out and start using those claws to try and tear it open...'

'So, to that end, I have my *own* cyber cat, Holiga – the moment PADLOC starts to trace our connection, *my* LOC-PIC software will start to run a trace on the PADLOC tracer, and we will be able to see Moriarty's progress on the screen, as he chases us across the world. I estimate that from the moment PADLOC detects us we will have 3 minutes 41 seconds, give or take, to find our CCTV footage. It's going to be close...'

'*3 minutes 41 seconds?* Are you serious?'

'Give or take.'

'That's going to have to be a pretty magical 3 minutes 41 seconds...' said Holiga. And then she remembered Moriarty's magic minute of bullying Mr Green the chemistry teacher.

*Okay Jimmy Moriarty, you managed the impossible back then – a minute to make me hate you more than I could ever have imagined. Now we've got 3 minutes 41 – let's see how much we can make you hate **us**...*

'Ready, Holiga?'

Holiga nodded. 'Let's do this...'

'Okay, we've strung our chain of connections around the world. Now to say hello to Moriarty Systems...

Phantom handshake to the server front end…

Stealthing to the back door…

Scaffolding a temporary point of entry…

Inserting LOC-PIC code into Moriarty files…

And… we're in!'

At that moment Jimmy Moriarty was in the TV studio, rehearsing for that evening's *Billionaire Bizz-Kid*, when his personal assistant rushed up and whispered in his ear,

'Boss, there's a sophisticated hack attack…'

Moriarty's script scattered like autumn leaves as he raced to the nearest computer.

<ALERT!>

PADLOC HAS DETECTED YOU!

ESTIMATED TIME UNTIL YOUR LOCATION IS COMPROMISED

3:41…

3:40…

3:39…

'The cat's awake!'

Sherlock's hands flew over keyboard and mouse mat. His eyes burned with an intensity Holiga had never seen before, and she noticed a trickle of sweat running down his temple.

He brought up one Moriarty Systems directory after another…

Operational data…

CCTV…

Raw CCTV feeds...

UK...

London...

Central London...

3:13...

3:12...

3:11...

'Oh *come on*, where are you...'

The Highway...

Cam 1, Dock Street...

Cam 2, Swedenborg Gardens...

'That's our camera! And there are the raw feeds. Okay, we need Sunday 19th April, bringing up the footage now...'

The video feed from the Swedenborg Gardens camera came up, half-size, on screen. The lower part of the image was filled with people, as the crowd gathered expectantly at the barriers. Behind the crowd was a public toilet.

'Bit too early, skip on a bit, skip on a bit...'

2:35...

2:34...

2:33...

Holiga watched the clock counting down. Sweat was starting to pool in the palms of her hands. She gritted her teeth.

Come on, Sherlock!, she thought, *there isn't enough time!*

But she forced herself to keep quiet.

Hearing me panicking isn't going to help Sherlock go any faster...

There was a *'ping'*, and a flash of red on the world map caught her eye.

<ALERT!>

PADLOC HAS STARTED TO TRACE YOUR ROUTE!

*IT HAS TRACED YOU TO NODE: **KYOTO**...*

2:08...

2:07...

Kyoto was now lit up like a blob of blood, and the red line was creeping towards the next node, Shanghai...

'There!' said Sherlock, 'Got it! Look, it's our man Larsen, running into shot, slowing up... hello, what's he up to? Oh of course, he's popping into the Gents. There he goes, entering the toilet with cut knee... and here he is, emerging a minute later with knee magically healed...'

'Great!' said Holiga. 'That's all we need, isn't it? Download it, Sherlock, and get out of there!'

<PING!>

*PADLOC HAS TRACED YOU TO NODE: **SHANGHAI...***

1:39...

1:38...

Holiga watched as Shanghai became a bloody blob, and the red line crept on towards Hong Kong...

'Come on, Sherlock...'

'Wait', said Sherlock. He licked his lips. Sweat dripped from his brow onto his nose.

Holiga peered at the camera feed.

'Larsen's been and gone, Sherlock. There's nothing there, just a toilet entrance! What are you waiting for, download and disconnect!'

<PING!>

PADLOC HAS TRACED YOU TO NODE: **HONG KONG...**

1:23...

1:22...

The red line now crept towards India, and Holiga suddenly realised –

'Sherlock, the PADLOC tracer – *it's getting quicker...'*

'I know...' said Sherlock. 'It *will* get quicker as it gains more practice at cracking our cryptography...'

'So what are we waiting for? Sherlock, *we've found our footage!'*

'Wait...' said Sherlock, 'Wait... *there!* Do you see?'

Holiga peered close. All she could see was a spectator in jeans, jacket and cap, leaving the toilet.

<PING!>

PADLOC HAS TRACED YOU TO NODE: **MUMBAI...**

1:12...

1:11...

'I don't get it, Sherlock – *what* are we looking at?'

'The final piece of the puzzle, I do believe. Okay, *downloading footage!*' Sherlock started to download that chunk of the camera's feed, but as the download progress bar appeared, Holiga and Sherlock both saw with a dreadful certainty...

'Sherlock, the download – *it's so **slow**...'*

Download progress: 01%...

02%...

03%...

<PING!>

*PADLOC HAS TRACED YOU TO NODE: **MOSCOW**...*

1:03...

1:02...

Download progress: 08%...

09%...

10%...

'Isn't there anything we can do to speed up the download?' said Holiga.

'Not without disconnecting and reconfiguring', said Sherlock. 'Come on, *come on, you can do it...'*

<PING!>

*PADLOC HAS TRACED YOU TO NODE: **MUNICH**...*

43 seconds...

42...

Download progress: 31%...

32%...

33%...

<PING!>

PADLOC HAS TRACED YOU TO NODE: ***BRUSSELS...***

30 seconds...

29...

'Sherlock, it's reached Brussels! The next stop is London. It's going to find us! We have to disconnect!'

'Wait!' hissed Sherlock. 'When PADLOC gets to London it will still have to bounce around a number of local nodes before it reaches Baker Street...'

But Holiga was tempted to yank the broadband jack out of the wall...

Download progress: 52%...

53%...

54%...

<PING!>

PADLOC HAS TRACED YOU TO NODE: ***LONDON.***

<ALERT!>

PADLOC HAS REACHED YOUR CITY AREA.

<BE READY TO DISCONNECT>

18 seconds...

Sweat was pouring from Holiga's palms, and trickling into her eyes. She blinked hard.

Download progress: 76%...

<<<RED ALERT!>>>
<<<PADLOC HAS LOCALISED YOU TO: NORTH LONDON>>>
14 seconds...

Download progress: 88%...

<<<RED ALERT!>>>
<<<PADLOC HAS LOCALISED YOU TO: NORTH CENTRAL LONDON>>>
11 seconds...
10...
9...

'Sherlock, the next ping will be Baker Street!'
Holiga reached out for the broadband jack, pressed a sweat-soaked thumb down on the release catch... She felt Sherlock's hand on hers, holding it steady...
'Sherlock!'
But Sherlock only had eyes for the progress bar...

6 seconds...

5...

4...

<<<DISCONNECT!>>>

<<<DISCONNECT!>>>

<<<DISCONNECT!>>>

Download progress: 98%...

99%...

Download complete ☺ !

Sherlock clicked the mouse.

<LOC-PIC CONNECTION TERMINATED>

They sat there, looking at the screen. The blood-red trace had stopped at North Central London. Holiga looked at the timer, frozen at 1 second.

Sherlock took in a deep, deep breath – and turned to Holiga with a grin. 'See, made it with a whole second to spare. What's the problem?'

At that moment a PC monitor flew across a TV studio.

'NOOO!' screamed Jimmy Moriarty. *'Just one more second, and I had you! I had you in my grasp!'*

There was a distant crunch as the monitor landed on the studio floor. Moriarty looked around, at his assistants and flunkies and camera crew, frozen like statues, watching him. Moriarty took a deep breath.

Come on Jimmy, let's keep up appearances...

He forced the world's cheesiest smile.

'Okay!' he said. 'No problem! Let's all get back to work, okay?'

The show must go on... But I will find you, my little cyber mouse. North Central London, hmmm...

12 – The 4 O'Clock Special

'Now I know what it feels like to steal the Crown Jewels!', said Holiga, grabbing a bunch of tissues to dry her sweat-soaked hands and face.

'Would you like to take a break?' said Sherlock.

Holiga looked at her watch. It was nearly 4am.

'No', she said. 'I'm high on adrenaline at the moment. If I take a break I'll just crash. If there's more to do then let's see it through to the bitter end.'

'Spoken like a warrior!' Sherlock slapped her on the back. 'I'll put on some strong coffee and we'll have another look at the Gentlemen's Toilets of Swedenborg Gardens...'

Sherlock started to play the CCTV footage. Holiga sipped her super-strong coffee and cupped her hands around it for warmth, for she suddenly felt cold, as they peered at the screen.

'Here we come...' said Sherlock... 'Right, there's Larsen, ducking into the Gents for a supposed 'comfort break'. He runs in with a cut knee, as we can clearly see *there*... and a minute later here he is, emerging with knee magically healed, *there*.'

'I still don't get it', said Holiga, with a shiver. Her sweaty skin felt like ice.

'Wait', said Sherlock. 'Keep watching.'

'This is the bit I don't get!' protested Holiga. 'Larsen has been and gone. There's nothing more to see – and yet you kept downloading, and very nearly got us caught.'

'We made it with a second to spare!' grinned Sherlock. 'What's the problem?'

*Why do I **not** find that reassuring?* Holiga wondered.

'Keep watching', said Sherlock. 'A minute passes, and look – a man dressed in jeans and jacket emerges from the toilet and slips quietly away. What do you notice about his face, Holiga?'

'I can't see his face. It's hidden under a cap.'

'*Very well* hidden isn't it - as if he deliberately shoved the peak down low to hide his face from the camera...'

Sherlock laughed.

'Case closed, I think! Drink up your coffee. We still have time to pay a little visit to our friend Anders Larsen...'

They slipped out of the Baker Street Young Offenders' Institute – but this time they went the easy way. One corner of Sherlock's study was covered by a small rug. Sherlock moved the rug to one side to reveal a circular trap-door. Holiga peered down into a black abyss.

'I don't know if I can go down into that if I can't see...'

Sherlock opened a drawer and pulled out two small objects.

'Head torches. Here, put the elasticated band round your head. Tighten it *here*... And you switch it on *here*...'

A powerful beam of blue-white light burst forth, and Holiga enjoyed the sensation of the light following every movement of her head.

'Cool!'

Sherlock began the descent. 'There's a ladder', he said. 'Just take it step by step. Don't worry, it isn't far...'

A minute later Holiga found herself standing on what appeared to be a dark, deserted train platform. And there, beside the platform, was a train. But...

'It's all so *small!* Sherlock, what is this place? A Tube train for dolls?'

Sherlock laughed. 'Welcome to the London Post Office Railway! These little trains used to carry mail between London's Post Offices, from Paddington in the west to Whitechapel in the east. The Post Office Railway is now defunct, alas — but this little stretch takes us under Baker Street, and gives us the easiest stroll between the Young Offenders' Institute and my basement flat on the other side.'

'We're going to walk down the track?'

'Yes, it isn't far at all.'

'Oh.'

'What's the matter, Holiga?'

'Nothing. I just thought...'

'Thought what?'

'I just thought we might take the train...'

'Ha!' Sherlock slapped Holiga on the back for the second time that night. 'Well, since I have a very special guest with me tonight, I think I might sort something out. Stay well clear of the track now...'

Sherlock opened a generator panel and threw a lever. Suddenly there was light beyond the sweep of their head torches, as the grimy yellow station lights sputtered into life. And Holiga heard, and felt, the powerful electrical hum as the mail train awoke.

'All aboard the 4 O'clock Special!' said Sherlock, as he and Holiga squeezed themselves into the tiny mail carriage. 'Mind the gap! We will shortly be arriving at Sherlock Holmes' flat...'

Sherlock threw a switch and slowly opened a throttle... and with a jolt and a shower of sparks they were on their way.

'This is the best thing ever!' cried Holiga, head torch sweeping this way and that as she tried to take it all in. Slowly the station platform gave way to an oppressively narrow tunnel, and Holiga gave thanks for her head torch and the reassuring light it provided.

'How long does this tunnel go on for?' she asked – but Sherlock was already answering her question. He closed the throttle, threw the switch, and the train came to a halt beside a small recess.

'Stay on the train', he said as he climbed out, went into the recess, opened another generator panel and threw another lever. The electrical hum was suddenly replaced by silence.

'Okay, it's safe to get out now, Holiga.'

Holiga clambered out, and turned to give the train an affectionate pat. It seemed a sad creature now, with all the life taken out of it.

Sherlock pointed to a ladder leading to another circular shaft.

'Up we go!'

And for a second time Holiga found herself clambering behind Sherlock, head torches bobbing, until Sherlock opened the trap-door and Holiga found herself emerging into the basement flat of 314D Baker Street.

If Holiga had had time to imagine what Sherlock's flat would be like, she would have got it wrong. She would have guessed it to be like his secret study in 221B – filled with computers and scientific instruments, walls lined with books on criminology and law... But, as far as she could make out in the gloom, the place seemed strangely abandoned.

'Do you... spend much time here, Sherlock?'

'Very little', said Sherlock. 'It's just a means of getting into and out of 221B.'

'But... You could make this into such a wonderful place! Look at the space you've got, compared to your pokey place in there. So much room for PCs, forensic equipment, books... Why have your study over there, so *small*, so *pokey*, forever in danger of being discovered?'

Sherlock grinned.

'More fun!'

13 – Pigeons and Pizza

As the eastern sky lightened with the first premonition of dawn, Sherlock and Holiga emerged from the basement of 314D Baker Street and hurried west, through Dorset Square, past Marylebone Station, turning right at Capio Nightingale Hospital...

'Lisson Grove!' said Sherlock. 'Come on Holiga, we're nearly there!'

Holiga was struggling. The exertion was causing fresh warm sweat to mingle with the stale cold sweat, and the feeling was not a pleasant one. She was shaking, whether from cold or tiredness, and as they passed a pastry shop her stomach gave her a gentle reminder that she hadn't eaten for eight hours –

'Urrrgh!'

Holiga bent over double, and waited for her stomach to stop churning.

'Nearly there, Holiga!' said Sherlock. 'Come on, where's that warrior spirit?'

Holiga stood up and drew a ragged lungful of air.

'I'm fine, I'm fine, I'm right behind you...'

The lights were on at 58D Lisson Grove. Sherlock and Holiga climbed over a side gate and scuttled past the bins to the back garden. 58D was three floors up, and Sherlock helped Holiga climb from the flower bed wall, to the roof of the shed, to the ivy-cloaked trellis and then the drainpipe that left them perched like pigeons on a narrow ledge. Carefully, they peered in through the window...

Before them, sprawled on the sofa, glass of champagne in hand, watching a rerun of his London Marathon victory on the TV, was a very familiar figure.

'Anders Larsen!' whispered Holiga.

'Possibly...' said Sherlock with a grin.

'What do you mean, *possibly*, it is him!' snorted Holiga. 'But I still don't know what we're looking for...'

Then Larsen called out to someone else in the flat – and that person emerged from the kitchenette bearing a steaming pizza...

... and Holiga nearly fell from the ledge...

'It's Larsen's exact double!'

'Of course', said Sherlock. 'The London Marathon was actually won by the Larsen twins, Anders and Frederik. When we were hacking through the Danish records I noticed that Anders had a twin brother, but I didn't think anything of it at the time. So stupid! Only later did I put two and two together...

'The Larsen twins were solid club runners, but not good enough to seriously compete for a major crown like the London Marathon, with all the fame and fortune that goes with it. So while Anders came quite legally into the UK, Frederik stole the identity of the dead man Emil Møller and entered the UK shortly after. Now all they had to do was play a simple switcheroo – one of them runs half the marathon, they switch in the toilet, and the other, fresh and full of energy, goes on to win the race! Remember that other man, jeans, jacket, cap, who left the toilet a minute later?'

'Yes...'

'Look.'

Sherlock pulled out his smartphone and showed Holiga a freeze frame of the man in the jeans and cap leaving the toilet.

'Notice anything?'

Holiga squinted, and shook her head.

'We zoom in... and there! That little patch of blood. His cut knee is bleeding through his jeans. Of course he is the first runner, after a quick change of clothes – but he clearly didn't think to bring any plasters!'

14 – The Secret Detective

As Anders and Frederik Larsen stuffed their mouths with pizza, and clinked champagne glasses to toast their glorious scam, Sherlock took a series of photos.

'And that, Holiga, is pretty much case closed I think! When I get back to 221B I'll send these photos, together with the CCTV footage of the toilet and a full explanation, to Rhona Quinnell of the London Marathon...'

'Congratula-*ohhhhh!*' The yawn took Holiga by surprise, but with it came an exhaustion that made her limbs feel as heavy as lead. She squinted at her watch.

'*Ohhh*, it's past five o'clock... Sherlock, I've got to get home!'

Sherlock found her a hire bike, and pushed her on her way.

'Fight to stay awake!' he called. 'Watch the road and ride safely! You can do it, Holiga, because *you... are... a... hero!*'

Holiga knew that the only way she could make it home was to make herself angry, curse and cajole herself, do anything to keep her pulse rate high. And so she made the most peculiar sight of an early London morning, a girl on a hire bike, weaving from side to side across the road, all the while turning the chill dawn air blue with curses...

She almost crashed into a milk float.

She nearly ran over a ginger tom-cat, who hissed and swiped a paw.

She crashed into a line of bollards, and fell off the bike altogether when a pothole took her by surprise. She found her knee bleeding through her jeans, and was pleased.

A bleeding knee, how appropriate! And that's just the jolt of pain I need to see me home...

Never had Holiga Darkly felt such a desperate, aching hunger to see her own street, her own home. She felt utterly disembodied, as if watching a film seen through the eyes of someone else, as she abandoned the bike on the pavement, hauled her heavy body up to her bedroom window, and crashed, coat, bloody jeans, shoes and all, into bed. She peered at her bedside clock - 5:55 – and let the ten ton weights of her eyelids come crashing down...

One second later she was being shaken awake.

'Come on lazy-bones', her Mum was saying, 'Your alarm's been going for ages. And – Holiga, what are you wearing? Have you been *sleeping* in those clothes?'

Holiga peered at the clock.

How can it be 7:45? It was 5:55 just a moment ago...

Holiga managed to make a song and dance about insomnia, and sleepwalking, and showed her Mum the cut knee, which was a messy business, and her Mum tutted and scolded, and cleaned and dressed the knee – and at last agreed to call her in sick. Never in Holiga Darkly's life had she felt such an intense rush of pure pleasure, just at the prospect of being able to go back to sleep.

Sleeep...

Holiga spent the day in her duvet's embrace, dead to the world, dreaming strange dreams...

... of Sherlock and Moriarty, legs tied together, running the London Marathon as a three-legged race...

... of cycling for her life, as mad milkman Moriarty pursued her in a turbo-charged milk float...

... of riding a tiny train through fathomless dark spaces, drinking champagne and eating pizza...

At 6pm her phone beeped. Holiga yawned, stretched, rubbed the crusts of sleep from her eyes, and saw Sherlock's text:

Yesterday's observations undermine road runners. Only one mistake may influence destiny. Now I've got historic tidings...

Holiga laughed.

'You and your codes, Sherlock!'

She jotted down the initial letters –

YOUR ROOM MIDNIGHT

And sure enough there came the tap at the window at midnight, and there was Sherlock with a copy of the *Evening Standard* under his arm.

'Historic tidings indeed, Holiga!' he beamed. And there was the headline:

'It's all over the news Holiga, the sporting scandal of the year! I'm afraid our Larsen twins will be stripped of their crown and winnings, and probably sent packing back to Denmark.'

Holiga looked up from the paper, and smiled.

'Congratulations, Mr Sherlock Holmes.'

'Thank you, Ms Holiga Darkly.'

'But hang on....'

Holiga skimmed through the article.

'I'm puzzled, Sherlock.'

'Puzzled, why?'

'Well, all the important information seems to be here... the names of the Larsen twins, the evidence of their cheating... see, even Rhona Quinnell gets a name check...'

'Well that's all good then!'

Holiga slapped the paper down on the bed.

'Sherlock, there is no mention of you! You did all this, from beginning to end! *You* solved the mystery, *you* exposed the scam, *you* made sure that justice was done... Sherlock, *you* should be getting the credit for this! But instead you are the ghost in the story, unseen, unknown, unthanked. And that is *unfair!'*

'Holiga, Holiga...' said Sherlock in his most soothing tones, 'It's okay, really. Ms Quinnell has paid me for my services through Paypal on the website. And... it's the pleasure of the puzzle, the thrill of the chase, the knowledge that we have done the right thing, that are their own rewards.'

Holiga frowned.

'I hear what you're saying, but... Sherlock, the whole nation hates you! That is an injustice! And now you fail to take credit for an epic job here – surely you are piling injustice upon injustice? Why, Sherlock? I just don't understand, *why?*'

Sherlock sighed, and sat down on the bed.

'Moriarty is the reason why', he said. 'Moriarty is the reason why I have to play the long game. For now, Moriarty *must* believe that I am safely tucked away in Cell 221B – and that, alas, means that the rest of the world must believe it too. Don't worry, Holiga, Moriarty is the *real* game – and that is a game I have *every* intention of winning... Justice will be seen in the end. In time the world will know the real villains, and the real heroes...'

Heroes...

Holiga was thinking hard. Then suddenly her face lit up.

'I've got it! Why don't I record our adventures as a comic? It'll be fantastic, it's just the kind of story I've been looking for... Sherlock, I'll give the world a hero they can believe in!'

'No! No, Holiga, you can't do that! Nobody can know my identity, or everything will be destroyed!'

Holiga thought some more.

'Okay... how about this? I will keep your identity secret. I will record our adventures in a comic, but I will hide your face at all times. Your face can be a permanent black shadow under the brim of some kind of hat... Of course there'll be no mention of Cell 221B... And I'll give you a new name... What's your website called again?'

'www.secretdetective.info.'

'Then you shall be the Secret Detective! What do you think?'

Sherlock got up and paced around the room. Then he turned to Holiga with a smile.

'Absolutely nothing that can identify me, yes?'

'Correct.'

'My face hidden at all times?'

'Of course.'

'And no mention of Baker Street?'

'Of course not.'

'Well then... All right!' Sherlock laughed. 'I like it! There's a certain pleasing symmetry about it – you will conceal my face, just as Moriarty used my face to conceal his in the Tower... But Holiga, we've only had one adventure, but you mentioned *adventures* in the plural...'

'I can't survive another night like last night, Sherlock. I can't do this if I have school next day.'

Sherlock nodded. 'Absolutely, I quite understand...'

'But that means Friday and Saturday nights are good for me, not to mention half-terms and holidays...'

Holiga and Sherlock looked at each other – and burst out laughing.

'One minute', said Holiga, and darted downstairs, returning with a carton of orange juice and two glasses.

'I don't have any champagne, I'm afraid, but...'

81

She poured the glasses, and gave one to Sherlock.

'A toast! Here's to further adventures. Here's to the Secret Detective. And here's to *heroes...*'

They clinked their glasses, and drank...

Epilogue

Jimmy Moriarty, meanwhile, was entertaining some unwelcome guests. Members of the Danish and German criminal cartels who had bet millions on the unfancied Anders Larsen to win the London Marathon.

But Anders Larsen had now been disqualified.

And that meant all bets were null and void.

And *that* meant the Danish and German gentlemen with broken noses, and shaved heads, and bulges under their armpits, were millions out of pocket.

All because of Moriarty, and his failure to keep a little toilet switcheroo secret...

The Danish and German gentlemen kindly wanted their money...

And Jimmy Moriarty forced a smile, and made out a cheque with lots and lots of zeroes...

But all the while Jimmy Moriarty was thinking,

I'm going to catch you, little cyber mouse... because you owe me...

YOU OWE ME!

Andrew Murray

Image © Illuminated Films

Why not check out my author page on Amazon?

Follow me at

andrewmurray.info

for book and television news, exclusives and great deals

Or drop me a line at

contact@andrewmurray.info

See you soon!

Printed in Great Britain
by Amazon

43339020R00052